For my little sister, Sarah.

Green-eyed
GOOSE

A Boone Story about Overcoming Envy and Jealousy

BOYS TOWN
Press

Boys Town, Nebraska

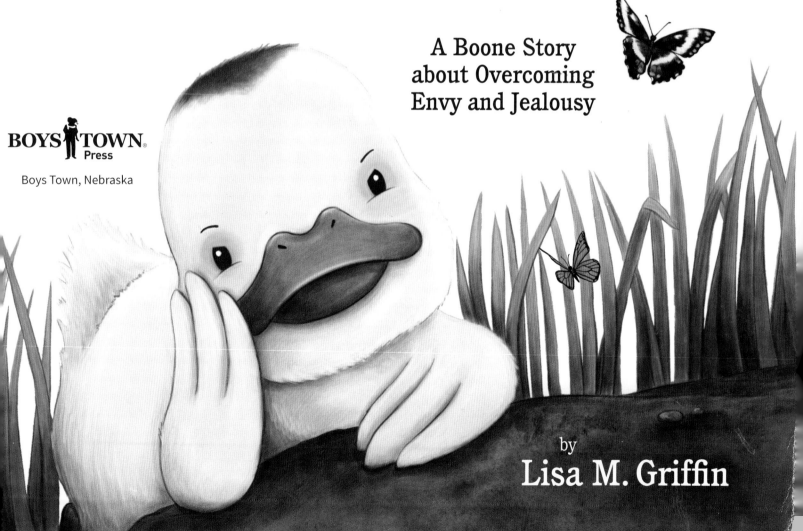

by
Lisa M. Griffin

Green-eyed Goose
Text and Illustrations Copyright © 2018 by Father Flanagan's Boys' Home
ISBN 978-1-944882-28-0

Published by the Boys Town Press
13603 Flanagan Blvd.
Boys Town, NE 68010

For a Boys Town Press catalog, call **1-800-282-6657**
or visit our website: **BoysTownPress.org**

Publisher's Cataloging-in-Publication Data

Names: Griffin, Lisa M., 1972- author, illustrator.

Title: Green-eyed goose : a Boone story about overcoming envy and jealousy / Lisa M. Griffin.

Description: Boys Town, NE : Boys Town Press, [2018] | Audience: Children pre-K - 4. | Summary: Boone is envious of everyone around him. But with help from his friends, he soon learns that instead of being jealous of what others have, he should remember all the good things he has and work hard to earn more of what he wants.--Publisher.

Identifiers: ISBN: 978-1-944882-28-0

Subjects: LCSH: Geese--Juvenile fiction. | Envy--Juvenile fiction. | Jealousy in children--Juvenile fiction. | Friendship in children--Juvenile fiction. | Emotions in children--Juvenile fiction. | Self- reliance in children--Juvenile fiction. | Children--Life skills guides--Juvenile fiction. | CYAC: Geese--Fiction. | Envy--Fiction. | Jealousy--Fiction. | Friendship--Fiction. | Emotions--Fiction. | Self-reliance--Fiction. | Conduct of life. | BISAC: JUVENILE FICTION / Social Themes / Emotions & Feelings. | JUVENILE FICTION / Social Themes / Manners & Etiquette. | JUVENILE FICTION / Social Themes / Friendship. | JUVENILE NONFICTION / Social Topics / Emotions & Feelings. | JUVENILE NONFICTION / Social Topics / Friendship. | EDUCATION / Counseling / General. | SELF-HELP / Communication & Social Skills. | SELF-HELP / Emotions.

Classification: LCC: PZ7.1.G754 G74 2018 | DDC: [E]--dc23

Printed in the United States
10 9 8 7 6 5 4 3 2 1

Boys Town Press is the publishing division of Boys Town, a national organization serving children and families.

Boone watched his brother Finn begin to fly.

3

"Why is he always first?"
Boone groaned.

"First to hatch.

First to dunk.

And now he is first to fly."

"WOW!
Look how high he is!"

"Yay,
Finn!"

5

"It's not fair!"
Boone said, as he plopped down on the grass.

6

"WOOHOO!"

Otter called, as he launched
out of the water and flipped in the air.

"**Hmph!** I can't flip," Boone said. "Why is Otter so lucky?"

9

Boone didn't want to feel this way, but he couldn't
stop bad thoughts from popping up in his mind.

"Why can't I fly?"

"I am never first at anything!"

"I can't flip in the air."

"I am not good at anything!"

"What is wrong with me?"

11

"TIMBER!" Beaver hollered as a tree fell.

He chomped on a branch and dragged it to the pond.
Boone watched with envy, as Beaver paddled
along using his tail.

12

Boone imagined what it would be like to have a big tail.

"Why do I have such a little, fluffy tail?" he sighed.

Boone felt **sad**…
  and **grumpy**…
    and **confused**…

Boone was feeling so many emotions that he opened his beak and…

... he let out a
GREAT BIG
"HONK!"

14

"Geesh! What is taking so long?"

"I think I hear something!"

"What's the matter?" chirped Bird.

"I have never been **first** at anything!" Boone cried.

"Hmmm... who do you think is in there?"

"I can't **fly** or flip in the air!"

And I have a little, **fluffy tail!**"

17

Bird hopped closer to Boone.

"There was a time I wanted to be **bigger**," she said.

Boone never thought about being little. He would grow to be a big goose, but she would always be a small bird.

"Then I realized, why do I need to be big? I'm happy just the way I am," tweeted Bird.

19

Beaver lumbered
out of the water.

"I used to be so clumsy with my big tail that I wished for a smaller one instead," he said.

"A little help here please!"

"Silly, huh?

How could I build or swim without my big tail?"

Boone never thought Beaver wanted a small tail.

Otter rocketed out of the pond with a splash.

"I practiced every day to learn how to flip," Otter said.

"It was hard, but I am **happy** that I didn't give up."

"I could teach you, Boone!" he said.

Boone never thought about Otter
practicing his flips.

23

If Otter taught him, Boone would be the **FIRST** goose in his family to do one. Boone imagined teaching his siblings how to flip in the air!

"You almost had it that time!"

24

Bird, Beaver, and Otter had
given him plenty to think about.
With a wave to his friends, he
began to waddle home.

Boone thought about what he was **grateful** for.

"If I feel jealous, I should think about the **good** things in my life that make me **happy,**" he said.

Cozy campfires

Learning something NEW!

HUGS

MY HOME

My family and friends

Eating DOUGHNUTS!

Playing Goose-Goose Dunk!

Paddling on the pond

Hide & Seek with Frog

What are you grateful for?

Bedtime stories

Boone returned home and saw
his siblings trying to fly.
Flapping their wings, they
didn't get very high
before falling down.

28

Learning to fly was going to take practice, Boone thought, but it looked like fun, too.

So... do you know what Boone did?

29

He joined them.

TIPS for Educators and Parents

We all experience moments of envy and jealousy in our lives.

While we can't eliminate these feelings entirely, we can teach children early on how to cope with these difficult emotions. Learning to recognize jealousy can help children avoid low self-esteem, as well as feelings of aggression or loneliness. Below are a few suggestions on how to overcome envy and/or jealousy.

1. **Acknowledge feelings of envy/jealousy and let him/her know you understand.**
Try a "Negative Brain Download" and write out any negative feelings the child is experiencing. Discuss positive ways to overcome those feelings.

2. **Encourage self-acceptance.**
Talk about individual strengths and avoid comparisons. Reinforce how making an effort through practice, hard work, and/or study habits will lead to personal improvements. In the story, Boone discovers Otter practiced daily to do flips, which motivates him to practice and learn as well.

3. **Jealousy directed at a sibling or close friend is normal.**
Celebrate differences and encourage cooperative behavior. What makes him/her unique? Talk about special talents/strengths. How can these personal skills be enjoyed and shared? Otter offers to teach Boone how to flip, which makes Boone want to do the same with his siblings.

4. **Be positive and patient.**
Envy or jealousy can flare up when a child is feeling low. Discourage negative talk and verbalize positive examples instead. Go on a "Gratitude Walk" (like Boone) and together describe all the talents, skills, experiences, and people you are grateful for.

NOTE: Material jealousy is common in children. In *Green-eyed Goose*, Boone deals with non-materialistic instances of envy and jealousy. This was a conscious decision to encourage children to feel grateful for what they have, instead of what they do not. These same lessons can be used to help children overcome material jealousy.

BOYS TOWN.
Saving Children   Healing Families

For more parenting information, visit boystown.org/parenting.

Boys Town Press Featured Titles
Kid-friendly books to teach social skills

Hey Goose! What's Your Excuse?
Written and illustrated by Lisa M. Griffin
978-1-944882-18-1

FREDDIE the FLY -MOTORMOUTH
a story about learning to listen
Written by Kimberly Delude
Illustrated by Brian Martin
978-1-944882-17-4

FREDDIE the FLY CONNECTING the DOTS
a story about learning to read social cues
Written by Kimberly Delude
Illustrated by Brian Martin
978-1-944882-25-9

Downloadable Activities: *Go to BoysTownPress.org to download.*

A book series designed to help kids master challenging social situations comfortably and competently.

LOU KNOWS WHAT TO DO Doctor's Office
Written by Kimberly Tice and Venita Litvack
Illustrated by Andre Kerry
978-1-944882-26-6

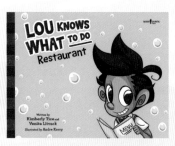
LOU KNOWS WHAT TO DO Restaurant
Written by Kimberly Tice and Venita Litvack
Illustrated by Andre Kerry
978-1-944882-27-3

LOU KNOWS WHAT TO DO Supermarket
Written by Kimberly Tice and Venita Litvack
Illustrated by Andre Kerry
978-1-944882-14-3

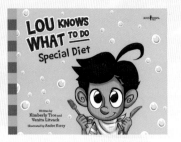
LOU KNOWS WHAT TO DO Special Diet
Written by Kimberly Tice and Venita Litvack
Illustrated by Andre Kerry
978-1-944882-15-0

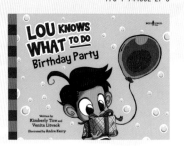
LOU KNOWS WHAT TO DO Birthday Party
Written by Kimberly Tice and Venita Litvack
Illustrated by Andre Kerry
978-1-944882-16-7

EMPATHY IS MY SUPERPOWER!
A story about showing you care
Written by Bryan Smith
Illustrated by Lisa Griffin
978-1-944882-29-7

MINDSET MATTERS
Written by Bryan Smith
Illustrated by Lisa Griffin
978-1-944882-12-9

Kindness Counts
a story for teaching random acts of kindness
Written by Bryan Smith
Illustrated by Brian Martin
978-1-944882-01-3

Downloadable Activities
Go to BoysTownPress.org to downl

BOYS TOWN® Press

For information on Boys Town, its Education Model, Common Sense Parenting®, and training programs:
boystowntraining.org | boystown.org/parenting
training@BoysTown.org | 1-800-545-5771

For parenting and educational books and other resources:
BoysTownPress.org
btpress@BoysTown.org | 1-800-282-6657